W9-AAD-461

Original Korean text by Bo Rin
Illustrations by Do Gam

This English edition published by Big & Small in 2015
by arrangement with Dawoolim
English text edited by Joy Cowley

Distributed in the United States and Canada by
Lerner Publishing Group, Inc.
241 First Avenue North
Minneapolis, MN 55401 U.S. A.
www.lernerbooks.com

ISBN: 978-1-925233-67-4

Printed in Korea

Insects and Spiders

Written by Bo Rin
Illustrated by Do Gam
Edited by Joy Cowley

The forest is always busy.
Let's find out what is happening.

Wriggle!
Wriggle!

Who needs this dung?

The dung beetle will make a ball.

It will roll the ball along.

Then it will lay eggs in it.
The egg hatches into the larva.

Dung beetle

Does the cabbage butterfly
lay eggs inside dung?

No, no!

It lays eggs on the back of a leaf.

The grasshopper lays its eggs
under the ground.

Most insects begin their lives as eggs.

The water beetle lays eggs
on the male’s back.

The Ichneumon wasp lays eggs
in or near the body
of other insect larva.

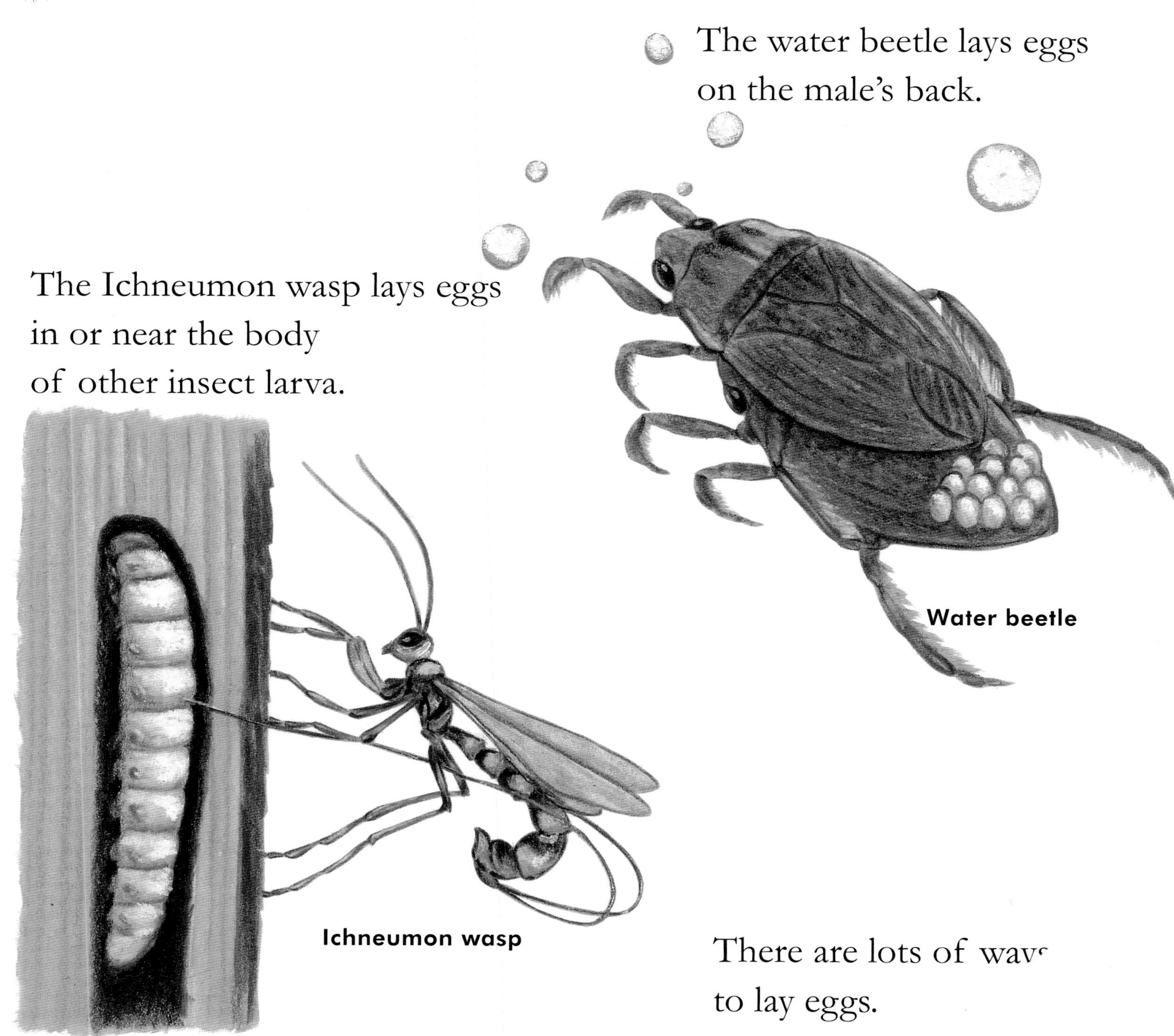

There are lots of ways
to lay eggs.

Who needs an old tree log?

Termites will make holes to build their nests.

Do these insects
make nests in old logs?

No, no!

Potter wasp

The potter wasp uses mud.

The bagworm uses bark.

Some use bubbles.

There are lots of materials used to build nests.

How does a water creature use air bubbles?

The diving beetle puts a bubble on its rear end. It takes in the air when it swims underwater.

Do all water creatures
breathe through air bubbles?

No, no!

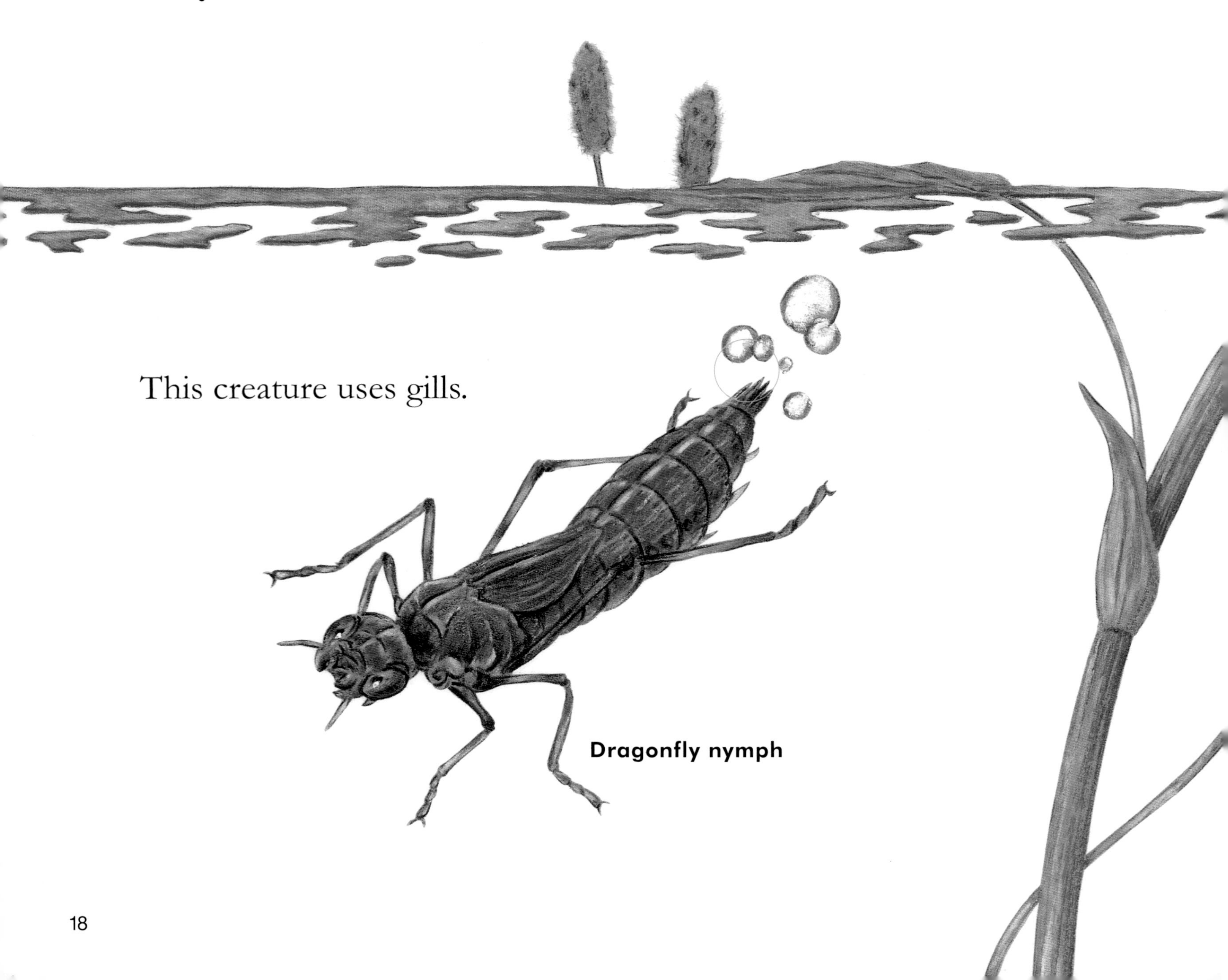

This creature uses gills.

Dragonfly nymph

 The larva stage starts when the egg hatches.

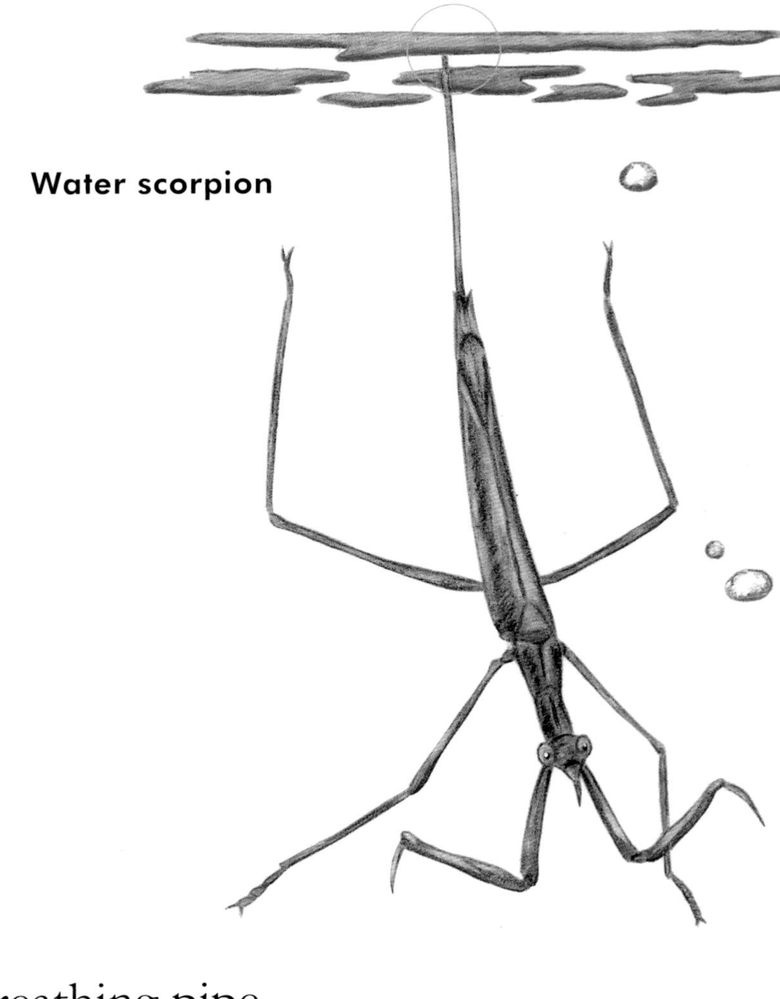

Some use a breathing pipe.

Swamp mosquito larva

There are several ways
to breathe underwater.

Who needs this leaf?

This caterpillar snips a leaf. It spins sticky threads.

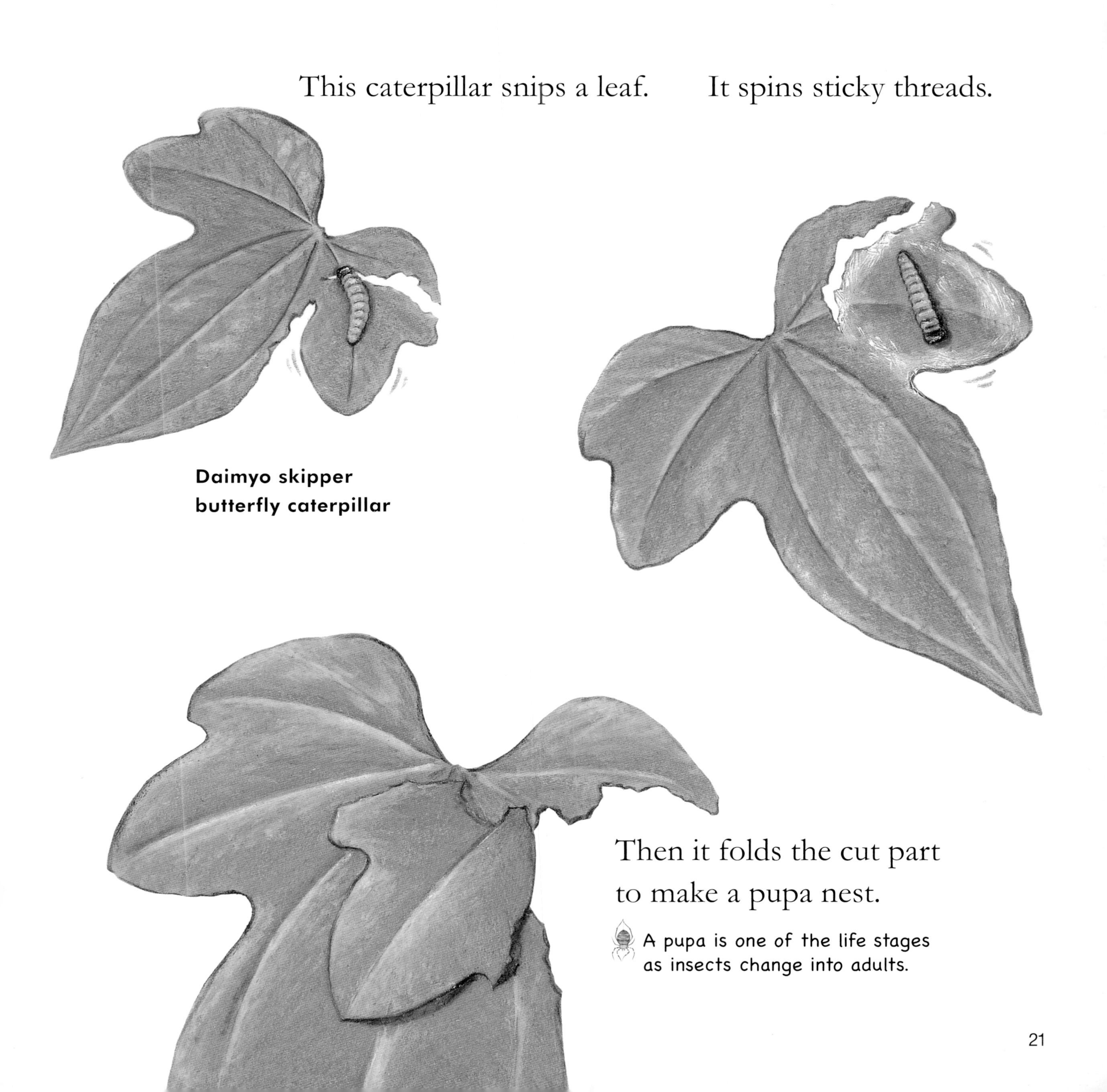

Daimyo skipper
butterfly caterpillar

Then it folds the cut part to make a pupa nest.

A pupa is one of the life stages as insects change into adults.

Do all caterpillars use a leaf
to become a pupa?

No, no!

The caddis fly
becomes a pupa in gravel.

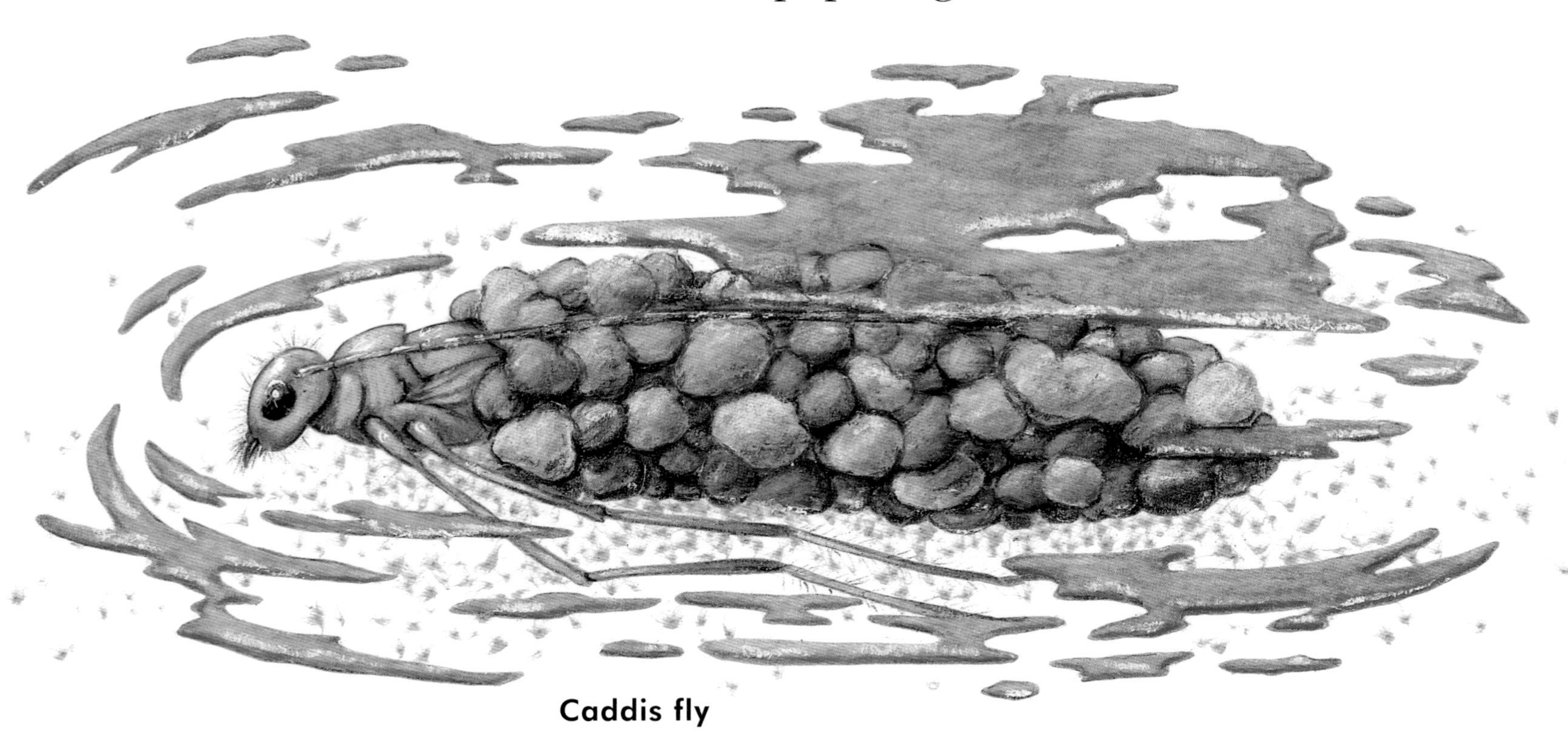

Caddis fly

Here is a pupa on a cocoon.

Here is a pupa in a tree.

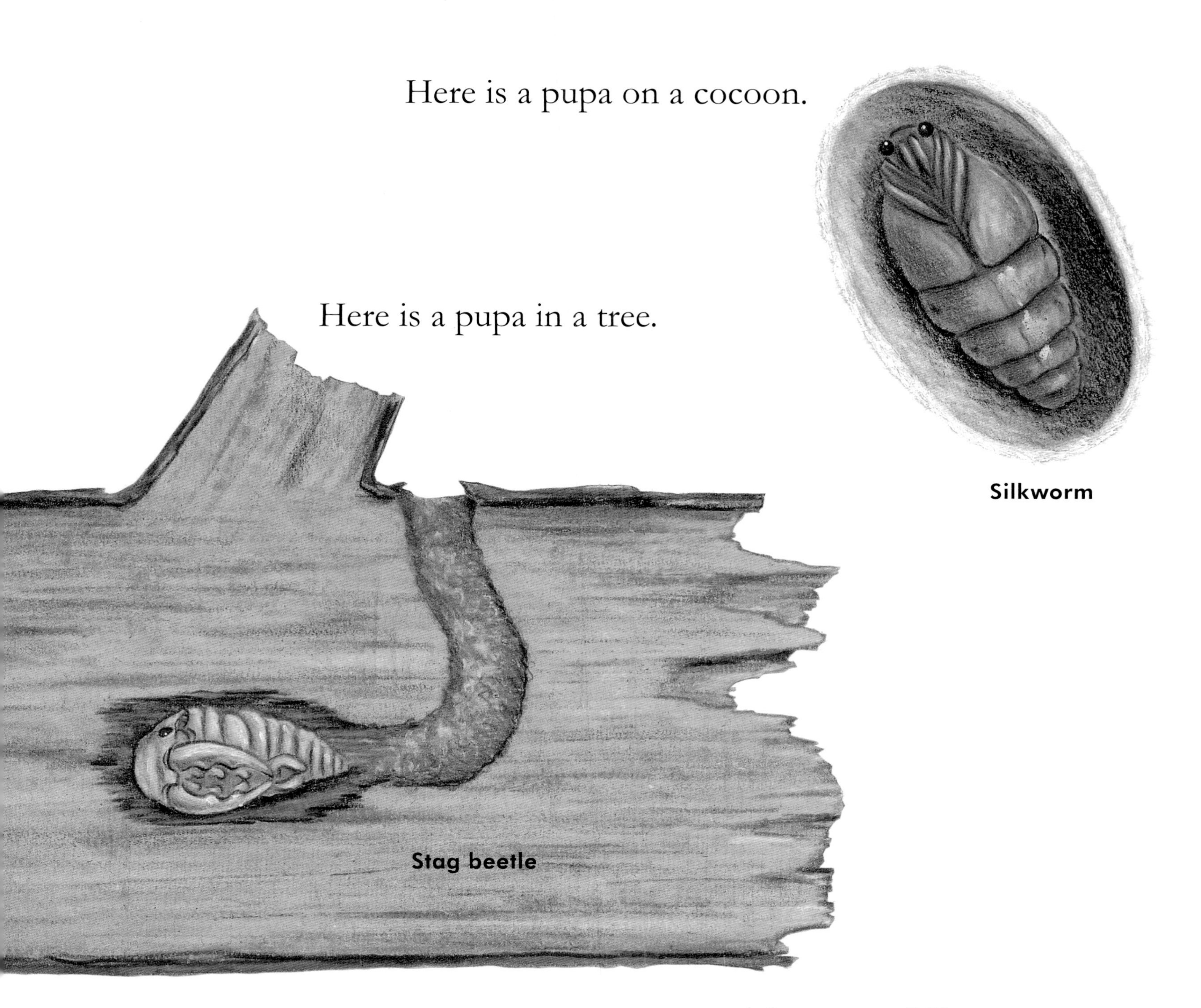

There are different ways
to become a pupa.

A long sticky thread
is useful for catching prey.

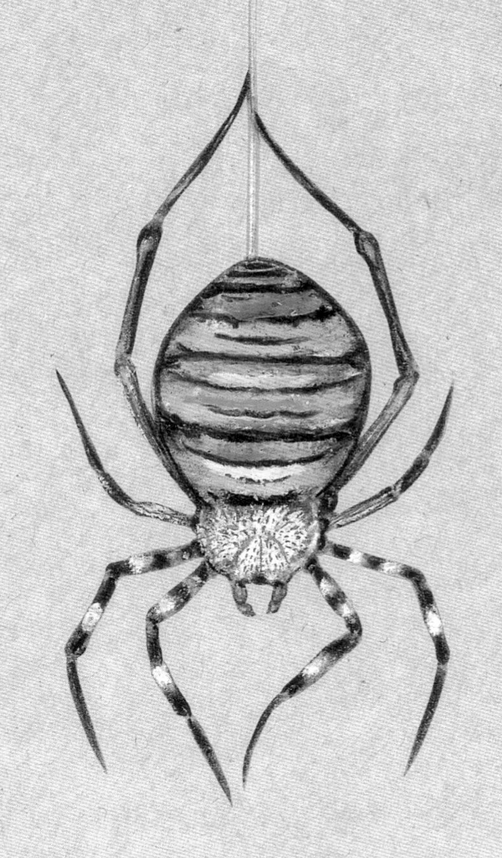

Is a spider an insect? No, spiders are arachnids.

The spider spins silk threads.

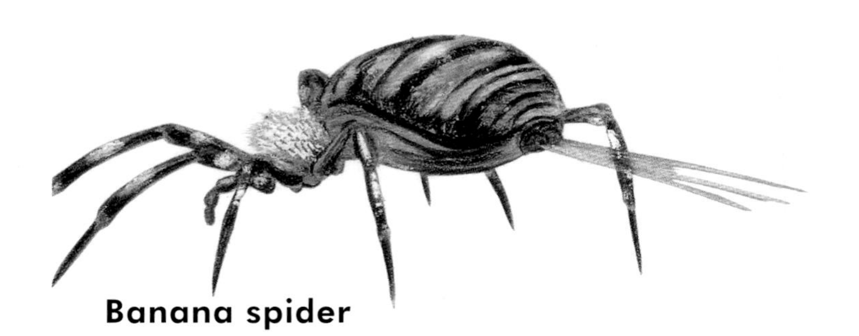

Banana spider

It weaves a web to catch its prey.

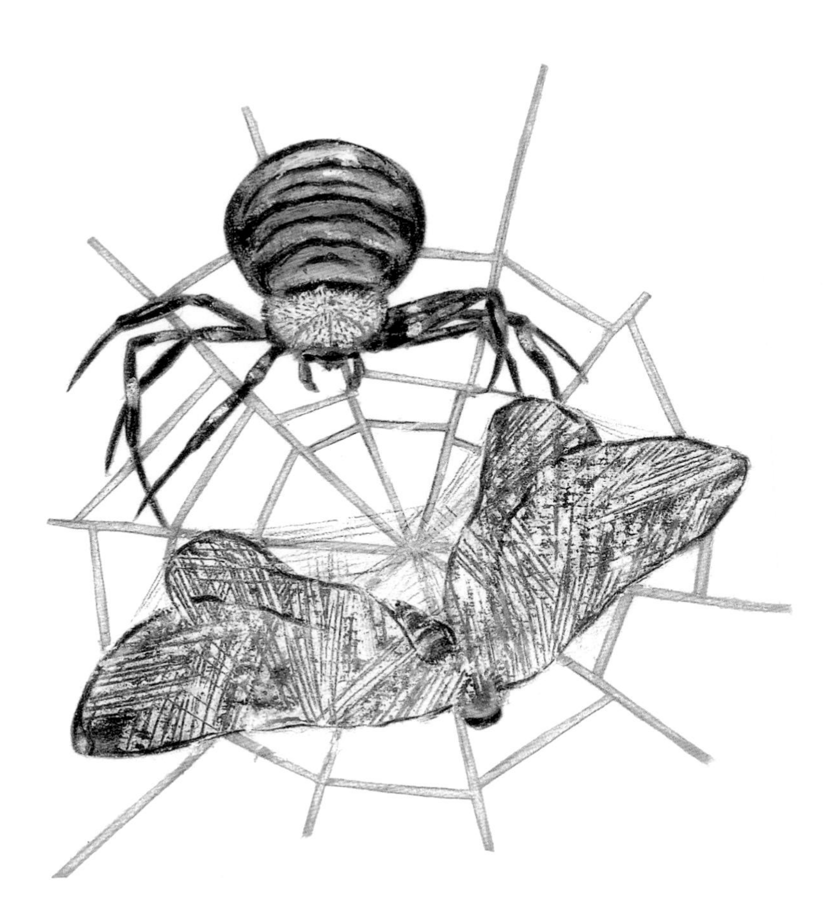

Other insects stick to the web.

Do all other creature catch prey by spinning sticky threads?

No, no!

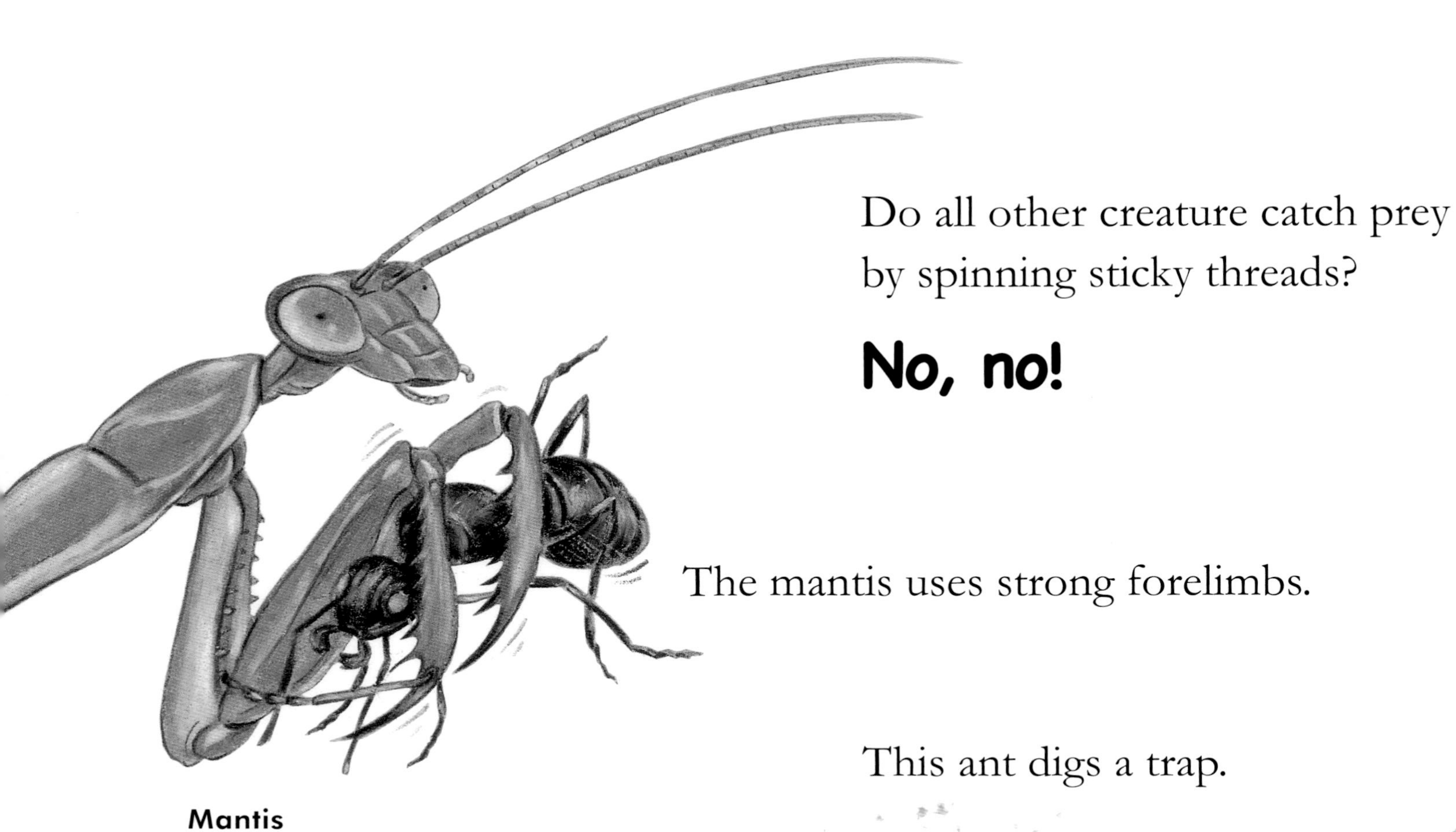

The mantis uses strong forelimbs.

This ant digs a trap.

Mantis

Lion ant

A poison stinger kills the prey.

Cicada killer wasp

There are many ways to catch prey.

The forest is full of movement,
small creatures working
with the tools nature gave them.

Buzz! Buzz!
Whirr!
Whirr!

Insects and Spiders

Insects are the largest group of creatures on earth. There are many types of insects and they have different ways of laying eggs, catching prey and developing into adults. Spiders belong to a different group even though they look similar to the insects. Insects and spiders use their habitat for survival and are well-adapted to their environment.

Let's think

What are the main characteristics of insects?
What are the main characteristics of spiders?

Let's Do!

There are millions of different insects and spiders in the world. Can you think of common names for various insects and spiders that begin with each letter of the alphabet? Write down as many as you can from A-Z and identify if they are an insect or spider. If you get stuck, you can use the Internet or library resources to help.

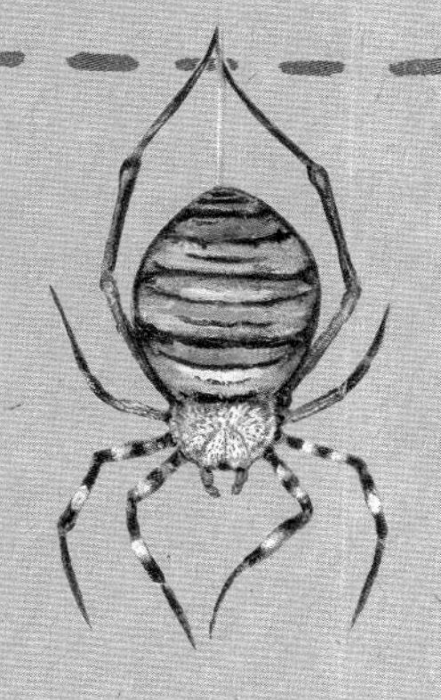

Difference between insects and spiders

Insects		Spiders
3 parts: head, thorax, abdomen	body parts	2 parts: cephalothorax (or head), abdomen
6 legs	legs	8 legs
a set of antennae	antennae	no antennae
Many insects have one or two sets of wings	wings	no wings